P9-CSC-157

MAXI, THE HERO

MAXI, THE HERO

by Debra and Sal Barracca
pictures by Mark Buehner

Dial Books for Young Readers
New York

Published by Dial Books for Young Readers
A Division of Penguin Books USA Inc.
375 Hudson Street, New York, New York 10014

Text copyright © 1991 by Debra & Sal Barracca
Pictures copyright © 1991 by Mark Buehner
All rights reserved
Designed and created by Halcyon Books Inc.
Printed in the U.S.A.
First Edition
1 3 5 7 9 10 8 6 4 2

Library of Congress Cataloging in Publication Data
Barracca, Debra. Maxi, the hero/by Debra and Sal Barracca;
pictures by Mark Buehner.
p. cm.
Summary: The further adventures of Maxi, the dog, who rides with Jim
in his taxi and becomes a hero when he chases and catches a thief.
ISBN 0-8037-0939-0 (trade).—ISBN 0-8037-0940-4
[1. Dogs—Fiction. 2. Taxicabs—Fiction. 3. New York (N.Y.)—Fiction.
4. Stories in rhyme.] I. Barracca, Sal. II. Buehner, Mark, ill. III. Title.
PZ8.3.B25264Max 1991 [E]—dc20   90-38329   CIP   AC

The art for this book was prepared by using oil paints over acrylics.
It was then color-separated and reproduced in red, yellow, blue, and black halftones.

To Florence Miller, a very special mom,
with much love.
D.B. and S.B.

To Merrill and Cynthia,
for your extraordinary enthusiasm.
M.B.

Jim drives a big taxi
And I'm his dog, Maxi.
Each morning we rise with the sun.
We greet our boss, Lou,
Have a biscuit or two,
Then set out to make our first run.

The day is just dawning
   And Jim is still yawning.
      We drive down the street to the pier.
There's no one around,
   And you can't hear a sound,
      But the toot of a tug that draws near.

"Can you take us uptown
    To the Hotel Crown?"
        Ask two sailors who've just come ashore.
"We sailed in from Tahiti—
    I'm Al and he's Petey."
        (Never saw a real sailor before!)

We drive up the street
And hear a drum beat.
We see a parade passing by!
The music's so loud
And there's such a huge crowd
Watching giant balloons in the sky.

It's already noon—
    Lunchtime, so soon!
        We head for Joe's frankfurter cart.
Jim always buys three,
    Two for him, one for me,
        And after, a blueberry tart.

We heard someone calling,
    "My meatballs are falling!"
        It's a chef with a tray of spaghetti!
"I'm late for a wedding,
    Across town I'm heading,
        And please try to keep the cab steady!"

Then we got quite a shock
    When we drove 'round the block.
        There were three boys who had the same face!
"We're triplets," they said.
    "Call us Ed, Ned, and Fred.
        Our ball team just took second place!"

We dropped off the boys,
    Then heard a loud noise.
        "Stop, thief!" a woman cried out.
And, in a flash,
    I made a mad dash,
        As Jim cheered me on with a shout!

A man stole her purse,
   And to make matters worse,
      All her groceries had spilled to the ground.
There were rolling tomatoes
   And bouncing potatoes,
      And peaches and pears by the pound!

The thief tried to flee—
It was now up to me!
I had to run faster to catch him.
I was close to his heel,
When he slipped on a peel,
And at last I was able to snatch him.

He gave me a fight,
But I held on so tight—
The police came along very fast.
The crowd yelled, "Hooray!"
As they led him away.
The big chase was over at last.

Next day in the paper,
They told of the caper.
My picture appeared on page one!
Jim patted my head.
"You're a hero!" he said.
"I'm proud of you, that was well done."

I loved my new fame,
    People knowing my name.
        "What a brave dog you are!" they would shout.
"That's him—there goes Maxi!
    And look, there's his taxi!"
        We'd hear as we traveled about.

As another day ends,
    We've made some new friends,
        Had lots of adventures too.
Tomorrow, there's more—
    Who knows what's in store?
        Come along, I'll be looking for you!

ABOUT THE AUTHORS

Debra and Sal Barracca are the owners of Halcyon Books, in which they work with many artists and writers of children's books. After riding in a taxi whose driver kept his own dog in the cab with him, the Barraccas wrote their first book, *The Adventures of Taxi Dog* (Dial), which was also illustrated by Mark Buehner. They will donate a portion of the book's proceeds to the Save-a-Stray Program of the Associated Humane Societies. Both native New Yorkers, the Barraccas now live in Katonah, New York, with their three cats.

ABOUT THE ARTIST

Mark Buehner was born and grew up in Utah and was graduated from Utah State University. A freelance illustrator, Mr. Buehner's first book, *The Adventures of Taxi Dog,* was said by *Booklist* to have created "an indelible canine character and a bright, equally memorable picture book excursion." Mark Buehner lives with his wife, Caralyn, and their three young children in Brooklyn, New York.

DISCARDED

12 PEACHTREE

J PIC BARRACCA   PTREE
Barracca, Debra
Maxi, the hero

DEC 2 7 1993

Atlanta-Fulton Public Library